CW01095382

Penumbra

Emily Steele

Copyright © 2016 Emily Steele

All rights reserved, including the right to reproduce this book, or portions thereof in any form. No part of this text may be reproduced, transmitted, downloaded, decompiled, reverse engineered, or stored, in any form or introduced into any information storage and retrieval system, in any form or by any means, whether electronic or mechanical without the express written permission of the author.

This is a work of fiction. Names and characters are the product of the author's imagination and any resemblance to actual persons, living or dead, is entirely coincidental.

ISBN: 978-1-326-62718-8

PublishNation
www.publishnation.co.uk

Chapter 1

I had everything I ever needed and more. Everything I could have ever asked for. When they say nothing lasts forever, they are pretty spot on. I got ill. And no I'm not talking about a physical illness or something like that. I'm talking about depression. An illness refused by many, but reality for so many more. Depression kills you just like any other illness. It takes away your morals, your respect and all the hope you have left inside you that gives you a reason to fight for yourself. "Get over it" and "it's just a phase" are some of the many phrases they chant at us as we sit there and feel everything inside us break apart. One by one you lose every part of you that makes you who you are, and the pain is crippling each time. Doctors and psychiatrists shove pills down your throat and make you go and see counsellors who are meant to tell you how to live your life. I'm sorry but if words healed people, no one would ever get hurt.

I spend days in my room staring at blank walls, looking for answers to problems that aren't even mine to be worrying about. I guess that's part of being a teenager though, over thinking, and the desire to make up scenarios in our heads just to make ourselves angry, when in reality half of them won't ever happen. But that doesn't stop us. Why? Because society is brainwashing young people to believe that they will never be good enough, that they won't fit in anywhere and that no matter how hard you cry for help, you're always on your own.

I, like many other sufferers from depression have arms and legs full of scars, pillows filled with tears and playlists full of broken hearts. I guess I am what you would call an outcast. I don't fit into a certain group or clique, that's okay though, I wouldn't want to be like those basic bitches anyway. Walking around in frilly little skirts, trying to attract the attention of a boy whose only intentions are sex. One thing you should know about me is that I don't do 'love'. Love is an evil and twisted emotion that is toxic to the heart and the well-being of humanity. I guess I've always been kind of a loner when it comes to relationships. But I don't think that you need a relationship to fully live your life the way you want to. You are born alone and you die alone and if you ask me, other people are just decoration into the black pit they expect us to call life. The less people you have in your life, the less people you have to judge you.

I am 17, so I'm still in education. Not by choice. If you ask me, we are all human guinea pigs being directed into a slow death that is a job that won't let us fulfil our overall goals. They used to ask me what I wanted to be when I grow up. I, like many other young hopefuls answered the classic 'princess' or 'fairy' and then when you realised that your whole life was a lie and fairies aren't real you started slowly realising that every job available to you is shit, you just have to choose the one that is less shit than the others. My class was full of the same bullshitting hopefuls with ludicrous dreams and goals that in this lifetime they are never going to achieve. We have the main pack leader, Jessica Brady. She is what I guess you would call the "queen bee" of the school. But if you ask me, the only thing she is queen of is the overpowering desire to be a spoilt little brat. She wears silly little boob tubes with hot pants that ride so far up her arse she probably needs surgery to remove them. She has thick, long, black hair that she always wears in a loose pony tail. Her face complexion is perfect. But with the amount of money her family pump at her, she's hardly going to be ugly is she?

Then there are her little followers. Holly Milton and Sally Clarke. I guess it's like a real life version of mean girls except these girls will probably actually achieve something in life. These girls unlike Jessica have short blonde hair. They dress like twins, which is weird because they are worlds apart. Holly is from New Zealand and she has skin whiter than paper, and Sally is from the Bahamas so she is naturally, strongly tanned with a thick accent that sometimes makes her sound like a man. Obviously these two were Jessica's little minions, but someone had to do the job that no sane person would ever dream of doing.

I'm not going to bore you with the others. To be honest I don't even know half of their names. School to me was a prison cell with disgustingly painted walls and teachers who marched around the room like royalty, when in all fairness everyone knows they get their silly little PowerPoint information off of Wikipedia. It must be really easy being a teacher though. Being paid to stand in front of a class and tell us how dumb we are and to restrain us when we try to use the toilets. The way I see it is that it should be illegal to stop children using the toilet. It's hard enough to concentrate in the first place with the boring lectures we are given at 9:00 AM, let alone with a full bladder. We've got no hope!

I remember how in primary school everything was so simple. You would play hopscotch in the playground until your legs became weak, and run around the field like an idiot just because you could. And now life is determined by popularity and how many likes someone gets on a picture, or who can sleep with the most people in the year. I think I make up for that small minority of the population who would give anything to go back to the days when phones weren't an accessory, but a luxury. When everyone would hang out together and have fun. That's what being a child is all about. When I was 12, my life was spent playing in the streets with my friends and watching cheesy kid's programmes on television, but nowadays, 12 year olds are drinking vodka, in cheap little grey tracksuits complaining about how bad their lives are.

No wonder so many people suffer depression or anxiety. You can't even walk into a shop without being paranoid that people are staring at you, and to be totally honest, with the way people's perceptions of teenagers are nowadays, if you think someone's staring, they probably are. Judgement is an evil thing that breaks people's self-esteem and confidence within their personality. But at the end of the day everyone does it and you would be lying if you say you never have. It's part of who we are. We as a community are so desperate to feel good about ourselves that we look to other people and seeing their flaws make us feel better about ourselves. Life is a poison that kills you slowly. It gives you hallucinations and highs where you think you are happy, just to then shit all over you once again. I guess there really is a circle of life after all.

Chapter 2

The fact that school is still 5 days a week is ridiculous. The government obviously didn't respond to my strongly worded letters. But then again with the amount of money schooling systems make these days with trips and expenditures, I guess it was kind of a long shot. I've spent the best part of 11 years in this shithole and I don't even know anything worthwhile to me at all. But hey at least I know the periodic table, and how to find the value of 'x' in maths. What more could you ever need to know in life? It's not like basic living situations and banking and account management are important.....bullshit. Maybe people would actually enjoy going to these hell holes if we actually benefitted from them.

My school was like all the other bog standard, poorly built, old structures. Paint peeled off of the cheap walls and the thin windows wobbled in the wind. All the doors were broken and nobody could be bothered to fix them, so we could literally have an intruder walk in at any moment and gain access to our whole lives. But that stuff isn't important anymore. As long as the teachers get their pay check at the end of the month that's all they really care about. To be honest, I would be the exact same if I was a teacher. Because let's be truthful, no one would be a teacher if the money was low, especially with this generation, I think I would request a permanent raise. Mr Barker was the headmaster of Modo academy, not that he was ever actually present in the building to account for such a supposedly well respected job. There is around 1,500 pupils in this school and I guarantee you he couldn't even name at least 5 of them. Having said that he probably doesn't even know half the staff he's got working for him, because you would have to be out of your mind to hire such utterly hopeless teachers.

I've always gotten into trouble at school. For stupid reasons of course. The teachers don't like me because they reckon I question their authorities too much. But I'm sorry, I'm not going to wake up at 6:00

AM to come in and spend half hour each lesson doing a stupid word search that they think will engage our minds. I mean who the hell sits in an exam and thinks to themselves "Oh yes, I know the answer to this! Thank you Mrs Rodgers for that word search we did in year 7." I remember I was in English once, and all this stupid teacher would go on about is how much she hated her job and gave us the most ridiculous tasks to write about that would ultimately make us fail our exams. Every other class was doing book reports and essays whilst we were sitting there being made to write a poem about how amazing pens are. I have to say, pens are a pretty useful invention but there's only so many words that rhyme with pen that you can think of before you start to go mad. I never went back to English after that lesson. I could learn more about English watching Disney Channel than sitting in those classes. It was after that incident that I started to get the reputation as a bit of a rebel child. Normally people have at least one subject that they are interested in, but none of them were what I wanted to learn about. I think that for GCSES especially in subjects like history, you should get to choose the time period you learn about to actually make you interested in it. How can they expect you to be enthusiastic about a topic you couldn't care less about? If you sit there bored your mind is going to wander and you aren't going to take any of the information in at all, and it will never make sense. By that statement you can probably tell that I've already failed history.

My life at the moment revolves around my increasing desire to hurt everyone I meet and push everybody away. It's cool though, I like it that way. It makes things more exciting. I am that bitch who makes people rethink their whole life plans and question everything that they believe in. I am a cold hearted girl with ambitions to make people as sad as they have made me. I guess you could say I am the way I am due to my childhood, but when I think about it, I was always destined to be a bitch.

Chapter 3

I am an only child. I guess you could call it a one night stand gone wrong. I spent the whole infant years of my life watching my mother drink herself to death and take pills until she was unconscious. I don't really remember too much about her though. She wasn't really around much. She died when I was 8, but by that time I was pretty much independent. She was a small woman with a grey face and Constant slurred speech from all the alcohol and drugs she took. She was weak, but she wasn't fragile. She was thick skinned and wouldn't take any crap off of nobody. Unfortunately for me, her family gave up on her long before I was born so it was only ever us two, sitting in a cold council flat with no electric, she used the benefits to buy cigarettes and to feed her other ludicrous addictions.

I was put into care at the age of 4. The problem was that mum insisted that I still saw her regularly. Not because she cared or anything, but because she became so immobile she needed me to go and get her more pills from the kitchen and more alcohol from the cupboards. I never refused anything she asked of me. She was a wicked woman who would do whatever she could to get what she wanted. To say I was scared of her is an understatement. The mailman stopped her service after I was born because they couldn't handle the abuse she thought was acceptable to throw in people's faces. No foster parent liked the idea about having contact with her and I was never in any place for longer than 2 weeks. When my mother died, I tried to get in contact with my grandparents but they refused to see me because they knew I would be broken and they thought I would be exactly like her. But I know deep down that I am much better than her. I would never give my children a life that they will grow up to not want to be a part of anymore like she gave me. Growing up knowing that wherever you go you are unwanted was a struggle. I think part of the reason that I don't do 'love' is because no one has ever showed me what it feels like to be loved. I remember I used to walk past a video shop which used to play movies where I would see children tucked in bed, with their fathers reading them bedtime stories. I always longed for that. Someone to teach me what it is like to have a family. Someone to make me feel like I belonged somewhere. But this isn't a video game, and you can't just start again when something goes wrong. No matter how hard you try.

Chapter 4

I woke up this morning just like I would any other day. I moved into sheltered housing when I was 16. It means I have to share a bathroom with six other people but anywhere is better than the sidewalk that I was forced to sleep on when my foster carers had too much of me. I can't blame them though, I annoy myself a lot too, but that's life and you have to get on with it. In many ways, I'm happy about where I am because it has made me strong and tough. I can take almost everything thrown at me and I love that about myself.

Due to placement issues my housing is over 4 miles away from my school, so I have to get up at like 5:30-6:00 AM each morning. I don't get enough money a month for transport to school so I have to walk. I'm almost always late but they should be grateful that I actually come in at all with the way they teach these days. The problem is that with the government's financial cuts they don't think I should get any money at all which is why my funds are so limited, but to be fair I didn't ask to be like this.

I guess that's the problem with living standards these days. As I walked through the door into the outside. The crisp, icy air hit my face like a thousand knives. It was January, so the temperature was just above freezing, and I didn't have a proper coat either because I had to spend all my money last month on replacing the toilet in the house, because someone decided to throw a party and it got demolished somehow. Apparently that's how things work these days. You don't even do anything wrong and you still end up paying for it. Instead I am forced to wear an old, black hoodie that doesn't even fit me properly and gloves that are so frayed they might as well be fingerless. Underneath that though was the basic school uniform. I got mine free when I started term because the teachers refused to let me come in wearing tatty clothes, even though they were the only ones I could afford. The uniform consisted of a white long sleeve blouse, a green V neck jumper with a blue 'M' on it to represent the schools logo, a green and blue checked, knee length pleated skirt and black dolly shoes. I always wore trainers on the journey though because they are more comfortable and let's be honest I can't exactly afford to replace the shoes if I ruin them. My school bag was an old, purple and white satchel from when I was little, with the words "live, laugh love" stitched upon it. I hated it but it did the job I needed it to and that's all I could have asked for really. I dyed my hair stormy blue when I was 15, that clearly went against the school rules but I didn't care. I believe that individuality is a key part to becoming at one with you inner self and I wasn't going to let a few prissy old teachers tell me what I should look like. We came to a compromise though; I refused to cut my hair so they let me keep it shoulder length the way it is, as long as I always make it look neat and tidy either in a ponytail or a bun. Normally I would complain but if anyone else dyed their hair they would be kicked out for sure, so I guess I felt special knowing that they bend the rules for me.

The walk to school was pretty straight forward although the path I usually take was swarmed by builders and construction workers so I was forced to walk along the main roads. I guess this would seem scary to most but in theory nothing scares me anymore. I've been so close to death so many times that it's a normal feeling for me and I feel so intensely numb all the time that if it killed me right now. I would be ready to die. Where I live isn't really all that busy, which is good but it has its downsides too. There's this part in the road where there is a massive pothole that keeps causing car crashes. But because the area is small the council don't think it is a priority to sort out at the moment. Ridiculous I know but it's just one of those things I guess. My walk to school tends to be just me and my music. No one in their right mind would be out at this time in the morning in this weather if they could help it. It's quite nice though. It's very peaceful and therapeutic to be alone with your thoughts. That is of course if your thoughts are not as depressing as mine. They say the human mind is one of the most powerful things in the world and they couldn't be more correct. Your mind controls the situations that you put yourself in and can be the difference between jumping off that bridge or choosing to go home and give life one more try.

Surprisingly I got to school on time today for once; I must have walked faster or something. It felt weird and everyone was looking at me like I was out of place. I haven't been early since year 8; I didn't even know what to do with my free time. I just stood there like a lemon waiting for the doors to open. And when they did I rushed inside to make sure I got the best seat in class. My first lesson was maths. Boring maths. Me and my best friend Toby, always choose to sit right in the back corner where the teacher can hardly see us. And yes I know what you are probably thinking. "She has a friend?" I have known Toby since I was 7; he like me was in foster care for a bit but his parents have sorted themselves out now so he lives with them again. Toby is a lot like me when it comes to life; I think that is why we get on so well. Toby has light brown hair that he spikes up to look like Simon Cooper from the Inbetweeners. He has bright blue eyes and wears thick black geeky glasses that make him look hilarious. His family are pretty wealthy though, so he always has on designer brands and wears expensive watches. That's what life is about these days, money. Your only as popular as you look, so if you look like a million dollars. People will treat you like you are worth a million dollars. He always has a girlfriend. In fact I think he gets a new one every few months, girls throw themselves at him. I think it's pretty pathetic if I am honest, like do people have no shame anymore?

The thing I like about Toby is that he doesn't ask questions. He just lets you do what you need to do and doesn't try and get in the way with anything. I could literally tell him that I am going to move to China and start a business and he wouldn't even give it a second thought, he would be behind me all the way. Heck he might even offer to come with me! Maybe I'll add that to my bucket list.

Chapter 5

You reach a point in your depression where you can no longer cry. Instead you just hurt inside constantly and there is nothing you can do to stop it. That is when you know you are truly broken. I sit there and watch people before me at school having fun and laughing with their friends. I can't even remember the last time I laughed, like properly laughed. It makes me so angry and upset seeing people happy. That sounds bad I know but I can't help it. I want to be the one who is happy. I want to be the one who laughs so hard their stomach hurts. I want to live. I want to feel like I am a proper teenager; these are meant to be the best years of our lives! But if that's true I'm not sure I want to see my next chapter if it gets worse than this.

Depression is like pins and needles. Its irritating, stops you moving properly and forces you to back down, and once you get it, you always know it's there. No matter how hard you try and forget about it, you always feel it until it goes away. The only difference is that depression doesn't go away. Not properly. It stays part of you forever, it just depends how much you let it affect you. But I guess when you reach rock bottom, if you know anything; you know it can't get any worse than it is.

Chapter 6

By now it had reached lunchtime. And if school wasn't humiliating enough, they made the people who were entitled to free school meals carry around a silly little neon orange dinner tray that you could spot for miles. They claim it's to be able to tell who gets free school meals and who doesn't, but I'm pretty sure they should know by the fact they have our names written on a wall in the kitchen. I'm pretty sure the reason we have uniforms is to stop people judging you on how you look and how much money you have. So why do they single out people in the lunch hall? This was one of my many thoughts going through my head as I stood in the queue waiting to be served. The canteen was no bigger than the size of a standard classroom, with tatty chairs and broken tables cluttering up the room. The walls were red, which I always hated because red doesn't match anything to do with our schools colours. There were never enough seats to fit everyone in despite having four separate lunch times for different years. You would see people standing in a corner trying to balance a plate without dropping anything.

The lunch menu was even worse. It was the same options every single day. They must get a discount off of the wholesalers or something. The lunch menu looked like this:

Food options	Student price	Staff price
Jacket potato with cheese	£2.40	£2.75
Plain pasta with cheese	£2.30	£2.50
Tomato pasta with cheese	£3.30	£3.50
Bacon baguette	£2.90	£3.00
Sausage rolls	£1.50	£1.75
Bangers and mash	£3.95	£4.10
Veggie burger	£2.65	£2.90
Still water	£1.00	£1.20
Sparkling water	£1.10	£1.30

Blackcurrant	£1.95	£2.10
Orange juice	£1.95	£2.10
Banana milkshake	£1.35	£1.50
Chocolate milkshake	£1.40	£1.55
Carton of milk	£0.80	£0.95
Apple or orange	£0.60	£0.70
Slice of toast	£1.20	£1.40
Pot of raisins	£1.60	£1.60
Multi-grain cupcake	£0.95	£0.95

Not only was the canteen ridiculously overpriced, but the people who gained access to the bursary, only had a £3.00 limit each day! So as you can probably guess we went hungry most days. It's not like the food was actually nice either. The sausage rolls tasted like cardboard, the sausages in bangers and mash were almost always still frozen and the fruit was well past its sell date. I always stuck to the same thing though; I didn't think it was a good idea to risk trying anything new. I ordered plain pasta with cheese, there wasn't anything else I could afford on the menu after that anyway expect a piece of rotten fruit and I didn't really fancy that. It's absurd that you can't even get a decent meal and a drink. I'm forced to bring in a plastic bottle that I have to fill up using the outside fountain. To be honest I try to avoid drinking as much as possible in school because the water definitely isn't fresh and I feel sick almost every time I drink it.

If all of that wasn't bad enough, the lunch ladies were much worse. They didn't use gloves for a start which I'm pretty sure is a violation of kitchen standards. They also never wore hair nets or anything and I'm almost certain if I kept all the hairs I found in my pasta, I would have made an entire wig by now! Why is it that lunch ladies are always so moody? I mean you are literally being paid to stand still and put pasta into a pot, there are far worse jobs out there so they could at least be polite and friendly. One thing I have no tolerance for is rudeness. If you are going to be rude to me I will be rude ten times worse back. I used to be banned from the canteen because I was apparently abusing the staff, but I'm sorry but if she hands me a furry pot of pasta, I'm not going to accept it. The amount of arguments I've gotten into with them other ridiculous things. I remember once I ordered my food as I usually do and this lunch lady gave me a pot with about 2 pieces of pasta in it and a mountain of cheese. I politely stood there and said to the woman "I'm sorry but I would actually like some pasta with my cheese. Can you please give me what I ordered?" well she was having none of that! "Excuse me young lady, you don't even pay for your meals. You get what you're given!" she said spitting all over my which can only be classed as a pot of cheese. And as you can imagine I was not tolerating her speaking to me like that. I told her how rude she was being and that she needs to earn some respect and that if she doesn't like her job there are many people the school can find to replace her so she should be lucky with what she's actually got. Anyway it ended up with some big issue and I was called into see the assistant head Mrs Saunders. She was as unreasonable as every other god damn teacher they have employed at this school. She asked me to apologise for what I said but I refused unless she apologised to me for spitting all over my food and gave me a free pot of pasta for the inconvenience because there was no way I was eating the one I was given. Well that never happened and I was given a formal warning about being rude and disrespectful to staff members

Funnily enough that wretched woman left not long after that. I could have thrown a party in her absence. I don't know why she left; my only assumption is that she was fired for her incapability of being able to serve a pot of pasta correctly. You probably think I am being over dramatic but let's be honest, if you get between a teenager and their food; it's never going to end well.

Chapter 7

I remember when I was younger; there was a little, old man who would always sit on the exact same bench in the park every single day without fail. I thought it was odd at first, but didn't give it much thought until, one day he wasn't sitting on the bench anymore, he was standing next to it looking at it for hours. I, being an obnoxious 13 year old, decided it was my business to go and ask the man why he wasn't sitting on the bench.

"Excuse me sir, I've seen you sit on this bench every day for years. How come today you are standing" I politely asked trying not to seem too nosy.

"Well my dear" he looked at me and sighed. "This was the spot I met my darling Francesca. She was beautiful. Hair brighter than the sun, a smile you could never get bored at looking at and hair that danced in the wind." He began to look upset.

"What happened to her, did she pass away?" I softly asked.

"Not quite. I mean she is gone, but she is alive in my heart. And always will be. This isn't some widow story that you read about in books and I can't stand here and pretend that everything was good between us. You see, Francesca loved me, but she also loved somebody else. Somebody better than me in every way. And she played with my heart until the day she died. Tell me young child, have you ever wanted something so much you would do anything to get it?"

"I can't say I have sir" I mumbled.

"Have you ever been in love?" he asked with a worrying look on his face.

I looked to the ground embarrassed. "No I haven't. I'm not sure love is something I need in my life"

He smiled. "Keep an attitude like that and you will go far. When you get to my age and everyone you love is gone, you're all alone, so the only person you need to love at the end of the day is yourself.

Giving your heart to someone isn't a good thing despite what the fairy tales claim. People rip you apart and then leave you with broken pieces; I spent my whole life broken. Don't be like me. Go and live your life how you want to, and if anyone doubts you, prove them wrong."

I didn't know what to say after that I just kind of stood there thinking about what he said. He walked off almost instantly and I never saw him again. I don't know the rest of the story regarding Francesca but I didn't feel like I was in a position to be questioning someone who is clearly still hurting inside for whatever happened between them. I think about him a lot sometimes, trying to think of what could have happened to him to make him feel so utterly and certainly against love. I think he in some ways is what has made me put such a high guard up to my emotions. Heartbreak stays with you forever, and is it really worth spending your life trying to impress someone who at the end of the day is going to leave you anyway?

Chapter 8

I thought about him as I walked home from school that evening. Because it was mid-January it gets dark at around 4:30 so you can guarantee by the time I've reached my home its pitch black. Today was like any other normal day except something felt different. Very different, and I couldn't quite put my finger on what it was exactly. It had been bugging me for ages and was driving me crazy. Funnily enough when I got home the feeling completely went. I continued with my evening as normal. Dinner for one. Then snuggled up in bed watching Titanic. I don't know what it is but there's always been something so fascinating about that film. I could watch it all day, every day and not get bored once. During school days I literally have no time at all for myself. Taking travel into account I don't get home until really late, and then have little to no time to prepare dinner and before I know it it's almost midnight and I have to get up early the next day. Weekends aren't any better either; it seems no matter what I do, I never have enough time for anything or anyone. Don't even get me started on sleep, sometimes I swear I don't get any sleep at all.

Chapter 9

Wow.

Just wow. I got woken up this morning by what could only be disguised as a farmyard full of police sirens. I don't know what happened or who did it, but all I can remember is being escorted out into the courtyard with everyone else who lived there. Baring in mind that it was around 3:00 AM in the middle of what can only be described as Antarctic weather, the sun doesn't rise until around 7:00 AM so I couldn't see anything, I was standing there in my thin pyjamas freezing to death. I sleep with an electric blanket to keep me warm but I don't have anything protecting me right now and I honestly felt like I was going to get frost bite or hypothermia. People around me were screaming and crying. I still had no idea what was going on. To be honest I didn't really care, I just wanted it to be other with so I could go back to bed and depress myself with how bad my school life is. But that didn't look like it would be happening any time soon.

Although it may be a small area. Where I live is very rough. Stuff like this happens all the time, and I guess you get used to the drama after a while. But this time something was different. I guess that could be what I was feeling earlier. I've always had inclinations before bad things happen, but that's normally like someone tripping over or forgetting their lines in a play. Not something as big as this.

A while went by and we still hadn't heard anything. They moved us into a café up the road to get some warmth. One by one people were being called out and taken, and before you knew it, I was the only one left. All alone. I began to wonder if I was going to stay there forever, until finally a police man came in and said "Are you Charlotte Leslie?"

"Yes" I said irritated. "I have to be up in a few hours! What is going on and when can I go back to my room?"

"Please calm down. We are moving you to another sheltered housing accommodation far away. .A car will be here to pick you up momentarily, by law we cannot tell you what happened until the investigation is over. Please cooperate with us on this situation. You will be starting a new school and due to the fact that we cannot get into the building to retrieve any of your items we will give you a compensation cheque to get the bare minimums"

"ARE YOU KIDDING ME!" by now I was screaming. "I HAVE TO MOVE AWAY FROM MY HOME AND LEAVE ALL MY POSSESSIONS BEHIND AND YOU WONT EVEN TELL ME WHY!."

"You need to relax ok. With all due respect madam, you do not own the property and strictly speaking you could be kicked out any time. I know it's not the best of situations but you're going to have to be the bigger person and accept that it is happening. The car will beep when it is outside"

He walked out and left me. I was too angry to even say anything back to that. I know he is right, this isn't my property and sheltered accommodation is almost never permanent, but really this is my life that I've built by myself being taken away from me. I don't even own a phone anymore to be able to let Toby know what has happened. How is he going to understand? What lies are they going to spread about me in school? And more importantly where the fuck am I going?

Chapter 10

The journey was long. In fact I didn't even remember most of it; I must've fallen asleep. I remember being woken up by the driver. We pulled up to an old building with white bricks and wooden doors with those iron handles. It was a big building from what I could see. Covering the face of what can only be described as a 'mansion' was moss. The windows were old, you could tell because they had that tape over them in a cross, like they did in World War 2 to stop them breaking. To be honest this place looked like one of those mental asylums you see in horror movies. In fact, the more I look at the details of this place the more it looks like one.

This must be a mistake. Why have I been brought here? I'm kind of hoping that when I get inside it will be different and just down to me over thinking again. I didn't want to get out of the car but the driver was becoming impatient so I had to.

Chapter 11

As I walked in the walls were painted black with scratches all over them. It literally looked like something out of a horror movie and I was the victim that everyone screams at their televisions telling them not to go into the house. But this is it for me, I have no choice. I need to find somebody to ask what the hell I am doing here, not only that, I haven't been to the toilet in hours so I am pretty desperate by this point.

The dark, damp floorboards creaked like a police siren. There was a long narrow corridor as soon as you walk through the cobweb ridden door. I remember standing still for a few seconds just looking around the walls for clues as to where I was, but nothing became apparent, so I decided to keep moving. After all, it's not like they would send me somewhere dangerous.

As I got to the end of the corridor I started to feel quite faint. After all I haven't eaten in hours. There was a big opening into what looked like a deserted waiting room, which makes sense if this was a hospital but surely its something else now?. All I could see was a rusty metal table up against one of the grey walls in the corner with a bell on it. I had no choice but to go over there and ring the bell, there was a few doors around the room but they all had padlocks on them so I didn't really know what to do. I rang the bell and waited patiently. I know someone heard the bell because there was a light turn on from one of the rooms.

This old woman walked out, dressed in a white tunic, white crocs, white gloves and she had her hair tied up in a ponytail. She had what looked like a Taser in her pocket. This was weird. Something is going on.

"Excuse me, I have been moved here due to housing accommodation" I politely said.

"Name?!?" she rudely snapped at me.

"Charlotte Leslie" replied, by now I was agitated.

She sneered at me, "Oh yes. I know all about you. Follow me to your room."

I didn't say anything to that. I was too tired for an argument and to be perfectly honest, who knows how long I might be stuck here. She directed through a narrow door which lead to a very brittle and rusty metal staircase. Kind of like the ones that you get in really old factories. Obviously I was going to have to walk up the steps but I was making sure I trod carefully and with caution. When we got to the top there was like a big hallway with rooms Had locks on them like everything else in this place, but I still couldn't shake the reason why they were outside the door, not being funny, but I am pretty sure its illegal to lock someone in their own bedroom without permission or even a valid reason. We walked along to a door numbered '121' she opens the door with a small little key and says to me;

"This is where you will be staying from now on. Do not ask questions because we don't spend our lives answering silly little girls concerns. The door will be locked all the time and you will be allowed out for meals and only meals. There is a buzzer on the door for emergencies, but just note if you ring the buzzer and there isn't something important happening, you will be sent down to the basement for the night or until we feel you have learnt your lesson."

"EXCUSE ME! I think you have the wrong end of the stick. I am here for the purpose of sheltered housing, I am not sure what you have been told or what you think you know is happening to me but it is wrong. So if you would please redirect me to someone in charge I would like to get this sorted"

She turned her nose up at me and let out a wicked laugh. "Silly little girl. There's no going back now. It's done and dusted, you are ours now!. Don't waste your breath screaming, no one can hear you. I am afraid you have been sectioned with us now. The police have signed it off. You couldn't even leave if you tried."

Before I could even say anything she walked out, slammed the door and locked it.

Chapter 12

I am absolutely appalled with how I have just been treated. This room looks like a fucking prison cell. There is a tiny, rickety little bed pushed up against the wall. No sheets or duvet or anything, just a towel and what looked like a bag of rice as a pillow. The only other thing in this room was a steel toilet with a broken seat. No sink or anything, no water supply, and all there was is a tiny window right at the top of the wall with bars on it.

I had no idea what the hell I was meant to do. I was trapped.

The walls were caving in on me and started to get a shortness of breath. I felt like I was hallucinating, hoping so much that this was all just a dream and that I will wake up back where I was. But let's be serious; I am not that lucky.

Judging by the fact that I had none of my personal belongings with me it deemed pretty destined that I wouldn't get anymore, well judging by this place, I wouldn't want to wear any of their tatty clothes. It's funny, I spent my whole life running away from things and making myself out to be independent when in reality, I have no idea what to do. I just slumped on the bed and, closed my eyes and tried to forget all of this is happening.

It was no use. Sleep couldn't save me now. This was something much different. And besides I was still bursting for the toilet so I had to get that out of the way. The toilet was really small in height. Like I'm pretty sure it's made for a child, I could almost sit crossed legged on it. And as for the supposedly 'toilet paper', it looked like tracing paper and felt like sand paper. I passed on this idea and took out a scrunched up piece of tissue I had in my pocket. The tissue had been in my pocket for months but I guarantee you it was ten times cleaner than anything in this room. Seriously though there isn't even any hand soap or anything like fair enough I wasn't expecting the Ritz hotel standards but I should at least get some basic toiletries. And where am I supposed to shower? There definitely isn't one in my box of a room and she didn't mention anything about being allowed out for showers or anything. I know that when I was little I didn't care much about showers and baths but now they are a necessity! And I can tell you now there is absolutely no way I will be using one of those group showers that they have in public swimming pools to save room, I may be easy going but even this is beyond my limit.

It's funny, when I used to daydream to myself when I was little, I never pictured that this would be the outcome. I didn't picture myself living in a mansion with the man of my dreams or anything like that, but even with my self-esteem I at least thought I would have a more dignified start to adulthood than this shit. God knows how long I will be stuck here. It's not like one of those films you see on the telly where the girl trapped always gets saved and lives happily ever after, the people who did know me think that I've moved far away and they can't contact me even if they tried because it's not like I'll be allowed any communication with the outside world. This was it for me. I could feel it. I will be stuck here forever and that's not even contemplating the way they will treat me.

There's something about this place that seems to creep me out. I don't believe in paranormal activity or the spirit world as such but I honestly feel like its haunted. In all reality no one knows, well especially I don't know what went on here before I arrived, anything could have happened I mean this clearly still is some asylum for the insane and incapable of independent living for the mentally scarred, so that alone is enough to make your skin crawl. The reason they lock up mentally challenged people is because they are a threat to themselves or others and to be honest seeing someone who is totally insane is very scary. These people can be so dangerous. This is what I am scared of. I am not like them, I don't have any blatantly obvious problems to be able to be compared to people that they care for here. How can I even relate to them? I don't know how their minds work and I certainly don't think the nurses will be much help with this.

As much fun as sitting in a room all alone sounds. The day wasn't getting any more exciting. Then there was a knock at the door, I think it is around lunchtime so maybe that's what they want me for? But to be honest I couldn't eat even if I tried. I feel sick to my stomach and the food here isn't exactly going to be nutritious is it?

Chapter 13

Clearly my assumptions were correct. Lunchtime it was. The lunch hall wasn't anything like I had imagined. If anything it looked like the food hall they had in Oliver Twist and I can guarantee you now, with the stench of this 'food' I definitely won't be asking for more. There was only 3 people in the hall. All sat separately and each with a nurse or equivalent by their side, probably making sure they don't try and hurt themselves with the cutlery or something. The layout was simple. Kind of like an old Victorian classroom. Rows upon rows of wooden tables and metal stalls that trust me have long since had their best days. The walls were painted white. Well off-white, but what do you expect. Hygiene clearly isn't their priority. Right in the middle of all these tables was a rusty water fountain. Clearly still in use, probably the only source of water they have here. Right at the end of the hall was a big table full of silver pots and pans that were clearly containing the food I was about to be force fed. I walked forward, towards the food. My eyes focused on what is in front of me. A nurse closely followed behind me, obviously making sure I didn't try and make a break for it. ha like I could if I tried!.

I was given a paper plate. I guess that's what they use here instead of actual crockery. They will probably give me plastic cutlery too. "Why do I have to use plastic and paper for my food when they get proper utensils and plates" I asked the nurse, gesturing at a young girl sitting near me. She had really long black hair and a pale face. She looked around 8 or 9 years old and wore glasses that sat elegantly upon her lightly freckled nose.

"This isn't a school cafeteria" the nurse snapped. "You earn the rights to use proper equipment. And until you prove that you can be trusted, you get the plastic stuff"

She nudged me towards the lunch lady. She violently slapped some brown mush on my plate. And with a smug grin she looked at me and said "Don't eat it all at once" bitch. She had greasy thick grey hair that sloped over her shoulders like a dirty waterfall. Not a hairnet in sight obviously. She had a very wrinkly, peachy face. I'm guessing she must be at least in her 50s.

She wore a yellow apron stained with what could only be 12 years or more of rotten food. She had a large build and short stubby legs. Not married of course. But that's to be gathered. This was obviously all i was getting for lunch so i walked over to one of the tables and sat down.

As mentioned before there was 3 other patients in this room, one being the young girl, and two others.

The first was a young man. For some reason i presumed that this was a women's only place, or that if we were with boys we would at least be on different wards. He had a slim build bony figure with long legs. The uniform is clearly the same for everyone, so like the girl he wore baggy, blue, thin trousers and a white long sleeved t-shirt. Obviously the t-shirts would be long sleeved, to cover people's scars and past. He was bald and had a gold ring in his left ear. I could only see the back of him but I'm sure the front wasn't any more pleasant. The other patient was a very large middle aged woman. Her clothes were stretched around her ever-growing waist line. She had a acne riddled face and tiny eyes.

"Are you going to eat that food or are you going to starve?" my nurse snapped at me. She was a snooty cow, who like all the others was dressed in those ghastly tunics.

"That depends, what's for dinner?" i smugly asked. Her look was priceless. But nonetheless i took my fork and took a taste of the crap smeared across my plate.

It was revolting.

It tasted like watered down soy sauce mixed with raw potato. The texture was lumpy and slimy and was hard to swallow. I pushed the plate away from me in disgust "I have finished my meal, id like to go back to my shoebox now"

"You need to get a hold of yourself young lady. You wont last long round here with an attitude like that. We always win Charlotte, always.

Chapter 14

As I lay down on my bed, the nurse's words ran round and round in my head. What did she mean about always winning? Why sound so serious? What are they going to do to me?.

Being scared is a compelling emotion that captures your inner capability to think and act fast in a situation that requires dramatic impulse. The word fear alone spears so many memories and heightens the drastic emotion of individuals to such an extent that it can lead you frantic and delusional. In theory, we tend to be scared most of things we cannot control or situations that will drag us down with no way of getting back up. When anyone ever asked me what I was scared of, I didn't answer the usual spiders or heights etc. My biggest fear is pain. I guess you could say I am to some extent scared of almost everything. Everything can hurt you. You aren't scared of the spider; you're scared of the bite. You're not scared of heights, you're scared of falling. I am not scared of life, life is scared of me.

My mum always told me of a story about when I was younger. She said "You were always a happy baby. But that made me sad. You were always learning things so fast and that made me angry. I wanted a child that would need me and only me, and you didn't need me. Not really. You were independent and I admired that but it also filled me with envy. no one wants to see someone living happily when they are in so much pain" the thing about mum was that she opened up when she was drunk. She told the truth and that has always and will always stay with me. I do tend to think how things would differ if I was the child she expected me to be. Would she have changed her ways? Would she still be alive? Would I have still ended up here?

Haha of course I would have. Happy families only exist in cases of extreme wealth and in movies. What constitutes a happy family though? Care? Love? Companionship? Bollocks. Being happy isn't something that gets handed to you on a platter and it doesn't become more powerful if you have more people around you than others to watch you succeed. You don't need anyone to make you happy. Fact. If you love yourself then you don't need anybody else to. Don't live your life for someone else. Its okay to live your life with people who aid your progress, but if all else fails it's not worth it. Nothing in the world can compete with yourself if you truly believe you are everything you want to be. Everyone has flaws and things they wish they could change about themselves. But that doesn't mean you have anything wrong with you. Your imperfections make you beautiful and I would never discourage anyone or anything just for a pretty face or a brilliant singing voice. Fake isn't beautiful, it's a false vision into someone's broken and deep rooted desire to be something they are not. Anybody anytime can save up the money and get plastic surgery because they think that they will do better in life or get the man of their dreams by looking like the latest celebrity. These surgery places are an inhumane way to make women feel beautiful. They say that they are helping people feel confident and secure within themselves but that is shut down by the fact that these procedures cost thousands of money which takes me back to the wealth prospect. Why can only rich people look nice, everyone should be able to have the same rights to life and its these people and these definitions of beauty that are making teenagers suicidal and making people feel inadequate because society teaches that beauty is more valuable than brains or anything similar. I have been denied access to a lot of things through my life due to the way I look. Scars and cuts are looked down upon and quite often used as something to mimic emos. You get judged so deeply about everything. You could have straight As and a clear criminal record but just because you have a tattoo on your arm on a unnatural hair colour, you are bypassed as an outsider and dismissed by companies and businesses so focused on the ambition to look good and be identified as a respected business that they turn people away who could make such a solid impact on the work that they produce.

Since when did it become socially acceptable to control a person's identity and pass peoples integrities off as phases and stages in life that contribute to personal stories and walks of life.

Chapter 15

A few days have now passed and I am still none the wiser as to why I have been put in this place. I have made a friend though. We have this support group thing where we have to confess our sins and control our demons, obviously does fuck all for me. I still leave there the same as I did when I entered. I remember walking down the corridor towards my ward and this girl asked if I wanted to help her water the plants outside, I quickly accepted the invitation because I hadn't been allowed outside since I have been here.

Her name was Laura, she was 22. She was admitted to the asylum because when she was younger she claimed that she could see dead people and no one believed her. She told me that she has been at this place for 15 years. She had short, spiky, red hair and hazel eyes. She had a slim figure and walked with a walking stick. She was the only one that I have had contact with the whole time since I came here. It was quite nice being outside though; I forgot what fresh air felt like. Because Laura had been here so long, she no longer requires being with a nurse 24/7, which meant that i was able to breathe without someone watching my every little move.

The garden was basic, a few plant pots dotted around. Obviously weathered and brittle, a couple of mossy trees in the distance, and about a mile stretch of weeds and nettles. I can see why they make patients do the work out here, it's like slave labour. To be fair I have never really been the sort of person to have connections with nature so this was all new to me. Not that it was anything I could tell I would be fond of. I tend to be a slacker in life when it comes to boring jobs, but this was an opportunity to get some fresh air, and I couldn't pass it up. Besides, Laura isn't exactly going to want to work with me again if I make her do all the work. And in all honesty I don't really want to give the nurses another reason to make my life misery. I am not an expert of mental institutions but come on, this is a little barbaric. Surely you are allowed contact with people on the outside, and since when were they allowed to practically lock you up for doing fuck all? This is worse than prison. Conditions there are better than this.

Laura didn't really talk much, not that I had a clue what to talk about if she did. She just kind of hums to herself. Songs i haven't heard of.. So I couldn't exactly join in. She mumbles to herself a lot but I can't say that surprises me. Being pretty much alone all day is enough to drive anyone crazy. Especially if you are already a little insane. I can't complain though I quite liked the peaceful silence, with the odd birds chirp to add effect. I didn't exactly know what jobs needed to be done so I just went and got a pair of scissors and started cutting down weeds around the building. They were children's scissors, so pretty much useless at cutting anything, but that's to be expected. I can't exactly see them letting us use shears or anything.

What I found odd is that these weeds weren't growing all over the place. It was like they had been purposely planted. But they were intended to be cut down. Maybe that's just something the nurses do to give people like Laura things to occupy their time with. Pretty smart I guess.

The one thing I do know about dealing with mental patients is that they require routine. Confusion isn't something they take lightly, so in theory if Laura does something once she will expect to do it again, hence why the plants were re planted. I know that they have a different mind-set but i hope they don't expect me to do the same things each and every day. Maybe once or twice I won't mind, but I have little to no patience, and it will not go down well.

The sun was beginning to set and Laura came and found me and said;

"Charlotte, we need to finish for today now. Its shower time before dinner and the nurses won't like it if either one of us is running late. Put your tools back where you found them ready for tomorrow. I'll see you inside"

She walked off abandoning me in the middle of fuck knows where. I guess I must have been wandering off with my thoughts because I don't even recognise where I am. I just walked in the direction she walked in and hoped for the best. Luckily enough I found my way back quicker than imagined. Gardening knackers you out, so I am kind of looking forward to the chance to shower. Laura mentioned earlier that on shower days you always get fresh clothes afterwards so I'm looking forward to being apart from these now grass stained pyjamas. I somehow found my way to the very vaguely labelled 'shower room'. Great. So it probably wasn't the typical shower I'm used to. I walked in. Dodging puddles of water to avoid getting my shoes wet. I couldn't see anyone else around except from a nurse so I walked in her direction. Weirdly this place smelt like chlorine maybe there's a pool or something nearby. This asylum is massive. There are loads of different sections and I don't even know if I'll get to explore the whole place. The tiles were yellow with black grout; every part of me is hoping that the black is intentional and not dirt.

"Wait here until the shower is empty" she said. "When you go in there, there's a basket where you put your dirty clothes in and the nurse will escort you into the shower"

"Okay?" I replied.

Not too bad I guess. At least I will be showering alone and even better thanks to that new regulation that came out a few months ago that nurses are not allowed to assist people in the shower. Thank fuck for that. Around 15 minutes went by and the nurse instructed me on where to go. I followed the corridor to this small room. Luckily enough, it was the nurse that I had with me for lunch so at least it was a familiar face. She went through the health and safety regulations which took ages and then told me where I needed to go and left. I put my clothes in the basket and walked into the shower. It was claustrophobic and murky; the nurse said showers are timed so the water automatically stops when it is time to get out. From what i could see past the steam was dispensers on the wall labelled shampoo and conditioner. Hygienic. The water was lukewarm and the shower pressure was ridiculously soft. The shampoo was bright orange and smelt like bleach. I tried not to think into the colour or smell too much as my hair needed to be washed and I didn't really have the time to be making decisions when I am being timed. I quickly rinsed it off and then applied the sticky conditioner to my hair and washed that off as well. It can't be that bad, I mean whenever I see other people their hair always looks in relatively good conditions so fingers crossed. Clearly shower gel was a luxury so that was nowhere to be seen but by the time the conditioner had left my hair, the water stopped. I left the room, grabbed an already damp towel off of the wall and wrapped it round me. There were supposedly fresh clothes hanging on a hook in the next room. Obviously the same crap everyone else wears but at least I won't look like an outsider now. They must have guessed my sizes. The top was baggy but I prefer tops like that. The trousers were a little tight around my waist and too short for my legs but that wasn't anything major. I walked out of this room into a corridor where I was greeted by a nurse

"I will now escort you to dinner. I heard you didn't enjoy lunch, but the food here is something you are stuck with. Don't try any of that refusing to eat malarkey, you don't want to be force fed do you?"

I don't know what has gotten into me. I just swallowed my rage and in silence took everything she said to me like it wasn't bad at all. Maybe part of me knows what she's saying is true, and as a matter of fact I'm starving so I don't exactly have the energy to argue right now.

The same 3 people were with me in the lunch hall, but that was to be expected with the routine system they clearly follow. I did the now familiar task of going to get my food. I'm stubborn so if I have nothing to say I will just ignore everything and everyone. I took my food and went to sit down.

The dinner looked at least a little bit more appetising than the lunch. It was some kind of curry, with white rice and a light yellowish sauce. My first thought was that it was probably some type of korma or something but it didn't taste anything like curry. It was really, really sweet and sour. The rice was a little hard but that isn't anything that's stopping me shovelling it down my throat. It could taste like literal shit but as long as it stops my stomach rumbling then I'll take it any day.

To my surprise I actually felt a lot better after eating. Nothing exciting was happening in the lunch hall so I just went back to my room.

Chapter 16

It's so weird how the smallest things can put you in a good mood. I mean who would have thought that basic things everyday people take for granted can have such a positive impact on how you feel. I have only been here a day and I am feeling somewhat relaxed. Maybe I am more easy-going than I thought I was.

My room didn't look too bad after I actually turned the light on and cleared all the shit away. It was warm, which was unexpected seeing as its cold outside and you don't usually expect places like this to be paying for heating bills, having said that, I don't think it would look to good if patients started dying of hypothermia. The thing that worried me about heat in these places was germs. Bacteria spread a lot quicker in heat and I am not prepared to start catching any illnesses.

As I rested on my bed staring at the light bulb hanging loosely above me, my mind started to drift off back to 'home'. Are they missing me? I hope so. I mean I'm not self-obsessed but it's always a nice feeling to know you are missed i guess. After all, I miss Toby like crazy. Bless him. Who is going to sit with him in maths and tell him funny stories like I did?. I hope he is okay

It feels weird being here, I don't really have anything to complain about all the time like I did at home. I mean this place is clearly a shithole but it's not too bad I guess. For once my mind feels clear, but I haven't decided whether or not this is a good thing yet. The last time I let all my thoughts in at once, I became severely depressed and in a place like this, I don't exactly need anything else making me feel alone. It must be at least 6:30 pm now, we don't have clocks in our rooms, well I don't anyway so I guess it's pretty much a guessing game.

A little while passed by, and my door was unlocked and opened.

"Miss Leslie, it's time to go down to reception to take your medication now"

Hold on.

"What medication? I am not on any pills or anything! I think you must be mistaken." i said maturely and without an attitude.

"Everyone here is under medication. Yours has already been signed off by a health specialist, you have two options. Either walk down there and take the tablets like an adult or we will drag you down there"

Fucking bitch.

Like the moody little teenager I am, I moaned and groaned the whole way there. I know in places like this they tend to give patients sleeping tablets, so perhaps that what they are giving me. Well I hope so anyway, I get homesick and will be lucky to get an hours sleep without help. I may be thick skinned but even I know when to shut up and do what is requested of me. And so I did.

The tablets were in one of those mini plastic cups you get given in hospitals. They were 4 different sizes and 6 tablets in total. 6! They were all green and red and one of them was a big yellow one. I am no expert but surely it's not safe to take this many tablets at once. By now the nurse with me began to look impatient, so being the pushover that I have now become I took the water, swallowed the tablets and went back to my room.

I have never been a firm believer of pharmaceuticals, I am pretty sure the last time I took any form of medication was when I was little and had to take Calpol, I hate the way medicines make you feel and the side effects aren't worth the risk. I remember having strep throat when I was 11 and I wouldn't take anything for it. I still got better though, yeah it may have taken longer but I avoided getting any other illnesses in the process. As for the stuff I have just taken, god knows what will happen to me. My body isn't used to having chemicals in it, so I'm bound to end up with something wrong with me. But I know for a fact that I will have to take these pills each and every day that I am here so I don't really have a choice about how I am going to feel. Is it weird that there is still a small part of me that thinks I will actually make it out of here?

Chapter 17

There was a park near the house when I still lived with mum. Well semi-lived with her. I was kind of in and out of that house when the carers got rid of me. This park wasn't anything special, it had a few swings, a couple of benches and a rusty old slide. But for some reason it always seemed to be my safe place to go whenever I was sad, scared or just needed somewhere to go. Where I grew up wasn't like a community or anything. It was six blocks of flats and a couple of poorly built houses. Mum claimed a load of money off of people and caused a load of hassle so they gave us a house compared to a flat. It's like they thought she needed more things to destroy.

One time, me and mum got into a big fight and I was left alone. Like I did every other time, I went to the park and sat in the usual place on the bench. Everything was normal, but something felt wrong. The air didn't feel right. The atmosphere seemed tense and I didn't know why. Obviously being my obnoxious self, decided it was within my interest to investigate the surroundings. Stupid as always. These street is not a very good environment to be in, the reason I go to the park at night time is because that is when all of the crack heads and alcoholics are passed out in their homes or patrolling the night clubs in the local town looking for their next score. This place was a safe as you could get at night around here. Well that is what I thought anyway. I walked around to where the slide was, this place is not very well lit so I used the torch on my phone. There was a puddle of blood all over the grass and no source of where it came from. What I didn't understand was that this area was covered in CCTV cameras, so if anything happened it would have been spotted straight away, dealt with and cleared up. But it wasn't. Where did it come from? The park was visible from my house so I would have noticed if something looks suspicious or odd in any way and so would the neighbours. But nothing. I didn't know what to do and to be honest I wasn't really in the best of moods after mine and mums argument. I walked away without looking back. I used to think that this made me strong, but it didn't. All that has done is prove that I am weak and selfish. I could have helped someone or something if I had just done The right thing and called the police or reported it. No stories or anything were released or any statements and the next day when I went back there was nothing there at all. I didn't tell anybody except from Toby. It's not like mum would listen if I told her and there would be a fat chance of her believing me anyway. Toby listened and helped me through the situation. He told me that he didn't think I was lying and that everything happens for a reason and to not feel bad about walking away. He helped me a lot in situations like that. Things I couldn't explain. He told me to stay away from the park, which I did. I knew that he only ever had my best interests at heart and I trusted him. He said I needed to get away from mum and move somewhere new which I did and he was always there for me. That's the thing about Toby, whenever I was worried or scared he was there. It wouldn't matter what was going on with his life or where he was, he always turned up out of the blue when I needed him. That is what best friends are for and I wouldn't change mine for the world.

I really wish he was here with me.

Chapter 18

Sadness comes in waves of desperation and loneliness. Its overruns your heart and causes you to feel pain in ways that even the strongest of painkillers couldn't take away. Whenever I cry, I always have a vision in my head of my problems melting away. Crying is the only way your eyes speak when your mouth can't explain how broken your heart is. Having a broken heart can be caused from so many things other than just a relationship ending. Why is it that we have associated being heartbroken with relationships primarily? It's just another form of instigating that relationships are the key to life, and what life is all about when it's not. You can be heartbroken about anything that means something to you. And it isn't in anyone's interest to ever make people feel any different. My heart has been broken by lots of different things. For example when I failed my maths exam in year 8. I was devastated and it really hurt my feelings. And you would look at that and think to yourself that a maths exam isn't something to be broken about or something that impacts your life enough to cause you great pain. But I can assure you that it is. Everyone has different priorities and emotions that one person's pinch is like another person's punch. It's the way we are brought up that makes us think that we need to act a certain way to certain things and it doesn't give us the freedom to make our own perceptions or feel how we really do deep down.

Chapter 19

I must have fallen asleep, because when I woke up it was bright outside and I could hear birds chirping. I just stayed in bed staring at the blank walls letting my thoughts take over me. Not that I had anything particularly interesting to be thinking about at this moment in time. The room was ice cold. Which was odd because the sun has been shining through my window for a while now so surely that would make it at least a little warm? I sat up on my bed and went to look out the window until my door opened. Same nurse again, it was obviously breakfast time. But no. Apparently I had a counselling appointment. I don't need a counsellor but I am taking this as an advantage because if anyone can get me out of here by seeing that I am completely sane, it's a counsellor.

I was walked into a little room with funny looking chairs all over it. There was a old-ish man sitting in a chair with a notepad in front of him. He wore thin glasses that had blue lenses in them. He had a semi-bald head covered with tiny tufts of white hair. He wore a white shirt and a pink tie with a brown waistcoat and faded grey trousers. He looked smart but not in a stuck up way. The nurse turned around, shut the door and left me. Alone.

"Hi Charlotte, my name is Chris. It's very nice to meet you. I will be your counsellor for your time here at Merecliffs institution. Please take a seat" he spoke politely and softly. I walked over to the chair that was furthest away from him and sat down.

"Why am I here?" I asked.

"It's funny, I was just about to ask you the exact same question" he smiled, but in a cocky way and that didn't sit right with me.

"There is no reason for me to be in here. You must know that considering you as a counsellor have access to all of my shit so you can see I haven't got any mental history or ever done anything to make me be in here"

"It's funny you say that miss Leslie, I am afraid what you are saying is not correct. Your file is packed with incidents and records that show quite the opposite of that".

"Bullshit, show me these files"

"We are not allowed to pass on information to clients, why don't you just tell me what you have done and we will talk about it. There's no need to be shy, I won't judge you" he is speaking in such a sarcastic voice, i could literally punch him right now.

"I haven't done anything in my life to constitute being in a nutty house! Whatever information you think you have is wrong."

"Calm down"

"Don't tell me to calm down! Everyone here just chats shit and puts things into my head which aren't true. You clearly have me mixed up with somebody else. I'm being made to take tablets that I don't need and eat food that tastes of literal rubbish, I've been taken away from my home and my friends and I don't know why so how about you give me some answers!"

"You think you are here under false pretences. Hypocrisy is a deadly thing that you should spite yourself for. You know exactly why you are in here and your lies are getting you nowhere."

"So you're saying I am a hypocrite now? I'd love to hear you explain this one seeing as we have only just met! I think I am done with this session now thanks. Goodbye".

I got up, opened the door and left. Who the hell does he think he is saying that he knows all about me. I haven't done jack shit. I'm done playing nice now. Clearly doesn't get you anywhere.

I stormed back to my room angry. Breakfast was off the table for me because it was my punishment for abandoning my counselling session. Lunch is mandatory though so I guess that is something to dread. All people ever do these days is make you think that you have done things and walk all over you when in reality it's all a pack of lies. Saying he has a whole file but then refusing to tell me any of it. He doesn't have anything on me; he just wants me to fess up to stuff so they can have a valid reason to keep me here. Too bad. I don't have anything to tell them. And even if I did, it wouldn't justify putting me in a place like this.

I saw something like this in the news once, about a man being falsely accused of having schizophrenia so they put him in a mental home. He was released after 15 years because on of his family members seized an investigation, schizophrenia alone is nothing serious enough to be sectioned let alone being wrongly admitted. You would think these places would have stricter procedures and ways of dealing with things since the uproar that the man's storyline caused, apparently not. I haven't had one health assessment or anything since being here. Probably because they know that they will find nothing wrong with me.

Like always I sat in the same position on my bed. This was becoming the new normal for me, and I can't say that it's a normal I am particularly fond of.

Chapter 20

Lunchtime was different today. Very different.

Everyone was happy. Too happy. It felt weird and I began to feel uncomfortable. The lunch hall was packed to the brim with patients dancing around to some kind of religious song. The nurses were dancing too and everyone seemed to be having fun. The lights were flashing multi-colour and I started to feel faint. I felt trapped. no one was here with me and all I could do was stand in the corner waiting for it to be over. Like is this some sort of joke? If you walk too fast in the corridor you get told off, but here everyone is dancing their socks off. Bodies swayed around the room like waves of tranquillity. I felt numb. Nothing inside me felt normal. And when I walked into the room nobody even looked up. I was in a daze, scary at first but then rather pleasant. I smiled and let myself go for a little bit. I wasn't even bothered that there wasn't any food here. I was relaxed, it felt like I was swimming, the air was soft and smooth and the floor catapulted me up and down in a trance like a trampoline. I always did ballet when I was in school so it wasn't surprising that those were the moves I went into first.

Chapter 21

I remember laughing. I laughed a lot, maybe too much. I woke up in my room. I don't know how I got back here or what even happened. Like I know I wasn't dreaming, and I had a big bruise on my calf that wasn't there before. Maybe I tripped or something and they brought me back to the room. But that still doesn't explain the abnormality of the situation that happened.

I feel sick. Could be down to hunger, or god knows what. I haven't felt particularly right since I took those tablets last night and I'm starting to convince myself that they have affected me in a way that I couldn't imagine. People at school used to be on anti-depressants and they would say they made them feel out of it, high almost. Maybe that's what they gave me. I feel like I am floating. But I am clearly not. Everything around this place keeps tripping me out. One minute you think you know what is going on and then the next it all gets flipped around and you go straight back to square one again. I feel like I am in one of those experiments they do to test people's willpower by putting them in strange situations and seeing how they cope.
Wait.
What if that is what is happening. What if I have been chosen to be a part of some test and they are monitoring my every move? Maybe that is why they tried to get me to say that I have done things, to see if being in a place like this makes you feel and act a certain way and live as if you do belong with these people. It all makes sense now. That is why I am locked up, so they can monitor me. And why I can't have any access to the outside world because they don't want anyone finding out. Maybe this is like a fucked up version of the Truman show. And I am the star. Yes, that sounds about right. I am the star!
Haha people at home are going to be so jealous when they find out all about my journey here. I'll become famous, and get to live the life

of luxury. They can't be keeping me here too long, they'll probably be done watching me soon so I can then go home and claim my millions.

I was called upon for dinner as usual. But I decided that I wouldn't be my usual boring self. I mean after all, I need to give those sick bastards something to be entertained about.

I strutted into the food hall, making as much noise as possible to get people's attention. If I'm going to get out of here, I either need to make them get fed up of me so they have no choice but to let me leave, or prove to them that I am incapable of staying under their poor care so they move me somewhere else.

I walked straight over to the serving lady. Put my plate in front of her, smiled and told her very arrogantly to fuck off. Her face was a picture, and not a very good one if I may say so myself. The nurse that I was with dragged me out of the room almost instantly.

This was working.

They were getting fed up of me over something as small as that! It will be so much more hassle to keep finding me alternative places to go for sure so this shouldn't take long at all. The thing with people in places like this is that you have to play them at their own games. And trust me, I wasn't going down without a fight. She lead me into a small room, where I was instructed to wait for someone to come and as she said "sort me out" That is the thing though. They know I am not insane or have any problems that would cause me to lash out at somebody like some of the patients here do, they know what I am saying is personal. And that is why I get treated differently. The door quickly opened, and in walked perhaps the most revolting woman I have ever seen in my whole life. She had a chubby, Caucasian body with fat rolls that hung down her stomach like a very heavy necklace. She wore an obviously too small for her work suit which was faded grey. The buttons on her blazer were ready to pop any minute and the white blouse she wore underneath it was covered in tea stains, and chocolate crumbs. I think I am starting to understand her weight issue. She wore low high heeled pumps which her fat feet stuck out of as she waddled around the room. She had thick lips that were stained with a lipstick that was half way around her face; her eyes were almost stuck together with the amount of mascara she has clearly slapped on. She had a skirt on that was not doing her any favours at all. She walked over to the desk in front of me, sat down and glared at me with those dirty green eyes.

"Do you really think that little stunt you just pulled did you any favours? Stupidity is an asset that we believed you were more intelligent than to grace upon our presence. Your morals are wrong and you will be punished for this behaviour. It was fun whilst it lasted though yeah? Don't worry though, it's not like anyone is going to miss you is it?"

"This is illegal. You know full well that I don't have any reason at all to be here. You need to let me go home, this is a diabolical way to be treated against my own human rights. What kind of place do you even have here? This isn't a mental asylum, this is just merely a place to make people think that they are something that they are not, how do you even wake up in the morning and get on with life knowing that you are limiting individuals chances at a proper life?." I am done shouting, screaming and giving a fuck now. I am drained. I can't let it show though, weakness is something that they prey on and I can't sacrifice myself to the devil until I truly know that I have no way out.

"This establishment is an apothecaries dream. We brew the medicines we give our patients and I can assure you we have had no complaints. Well having said that it isn't like any of the people who enter this place ever get to leave, alive anyway. Have you ever heard the story about the boy who cried wolf?"

"Of course I have, why is that relevant?" I looked at her confused. Her face still remained in the same shrivelled up mess as it had the whole time.

"You, just like the other hopeless people who end up here have already completed the first stages. Living your sorry life, with people sympathizing over you and giving you handouts just because you had some awful upbringing so you deem eligible for a life handed to you. The boy who cried wolf, gets his karma, no one cares for him and believes him after a while and before you know it its too late. Everyone will give up eventually Miss Leslie, even the ones who you thought cared will soon enough get their own life and forget about you."

"Why are you doing this to me? I haven't done anything wrong to anyone! I don't deserve this. Do you have no heart?"

She let out a crackling laugh. "You really think you are something special don't you Charlotte? People like you deserve to come and rot in places like this. Your mother is the reason you have ended up here, all our lives people like me pay taxes and funds into the government to pump money at drug addicts and poor excuses of human beings that think popping a baby out, gives them rights to have a life full of hand outs and free money for sitting on their backsides all day watching reality television. This is where we make our money back. The government pays us to house you and look after you; we will just call it reimbursements for the money people like your kind have taken from us hard workers yeah?"

Tears filled my eyes. "I am not like her! Nothing about me in any way will ever be like that woman, she ruined my childhood and now you are telling me that she is going to ruin the rest of my life as well. Do you know how many people these days claim benefits and I am being punished for this? Just because my mother was a waste of space doesn't mean that I need to be the one getting her repercussions for this. Surely there should be places and organisations to help people like me not punish me! I didn't ask to be born from her, I didn't ask to lead this life, and do you really think I want this?"

"Oh woe is me woe is me, poor little Charlotte. Mummy didn't love her so she wrecks the lives of individuals around her by depressing people with her problems, you don't understand the reason you are here do you? You are here because nobody else wanted you. No one could put up with you so they sent you away. And not one person has tried to contact you on that silly little mobile phone of yours. I'll keep that to myself though, not like you will need it."

I sat there in silence, staring into space. I didn't want to believe what she was saying but what hurts the most is that it kind of makes sense. Nobody probably has tried to contact me, as sad as it sounds, I may just have to deal with the fact that this is reality.

Chapter 22

After we had finished our 'chat', it was apparently time for my punishment. What the hell that means in a place like this I don't know. Obviously that wretched woman wasn't going to do any dirty work so it was down to one of the nurses again. We walked through a really long corridor and down probably the world's longest staircase, I remember at the beginning of my stay here, I was told that if anything happened, or I acted up I would be taken to the basement so I can only presume that this is where I am heading.

It was the usual nurse with me, It's funny, I don't even know her name. Probably no need to ask for it now, I doubt I'll get out of wherever I am going. The woman gave the nurse strict instructions to take me straight there and that she is not allowed to engage in small talk with me as that will reward me with company that I do not deserve.

Stairs have never been kind to me over the years, I almost always fall down every flight of stairs I come across, but I was holding on very tight to the rail to avoid accident. My hands were sweating, but I wasn't scared. The nurse walked down the steps slowly and I followed like her little lap dog. There has always been something about going down hefty flights of stairs that make me feel trapped and nauseous.

When I was 14, I tried to commit suicide for about the 8th time. Nothing worked and I wanted to get out of the world. I dug a hole in the garden, slit my wrists, and tried to bury myself alive. It seemed like a good idea at the time, a smart idea. But I guess I didn't think the whole thing through. It started to rain, and there I was, lying in an open hole in the ground. Drowning wasn't an option. It is physically impossible to drown yourself if you can get out of the situation. I wonder what would have happened if it didn't rain though? My arms healed as they usually did after a while.

I don't know what it is with places like this but my mind always seems to wander back to the past. Maybe it's because I am, in theory so alone and open to whatever thoughts come into my mind in this place that I haven't had the opportunity to mask these insecurities yet. This place is dark and full of a depressing atmosphere that preys on these thoughts my emotions are uncontrollable and I know for a fact that this will put me in a difficult situation in the long run.

By the time we reach the bottom of the staircase, it feels as if hours have flown by. To be honest, I'm just happy I don't have to walk all the way back up them. It feels like I am 50 foot beneath the ground, and the air is limited. In front of me all I see is darkness and nowhere to run. The nurse picked up a lantern off of the floor, lit it, and then gestured for me to follow her.

I stayed close to her, I needed the light. Not knowing where I am going is a fear of mine, and this place doesn't seem very friendly. I put my hand against one of the walls to help guide me along the corridor, the wall was cold and damp like a wet towel. The stench in the air was sharp and musty. It smelt like an old sewer, but that wasn't my main worry. The air was tight. It was cold, but not freezing. I could see little tufts of what looked like fog surrounding the now fading candlelight. I had to breathe through my nose because the air filled my mouth like candyfloss and tasted like acid. I walked with caution, fear of the unknown is a quality that I possess and until now, I never knew just quite how afraid I could be.

My knees were weak and I was trembling. We came to a sudden halt. I couldn't see anything so I just stood there frozen. The nurse made a rattling sound in her hands and began to, what sounded like, open a door. A ghastly creak pierced my ears and I began to feel faint.

"Wait here" the nurse said to me, and I heard faint footsteps disappearing away from me.

I was alone.

Chapter 23

Staring into total darkness can make your mind hallucinate, and before you know it, you're seeing things. I must have been waiting here for at least 45 minutes now, and I have the biggest migraine in the world. The thing with complete darkness is that your eyes strain intensely to try and make out things in your surroundings to try and help calm your fear. Nothing could be made out, not even a single shadow. Creepy right? The temperature was still just above freezing, but my body seemed used to it. My face felt numb, but not in a painful way. My legs were still shaking, and I began to feel achy after a while. I debated sitting down for ages before I finally gave up and slumped to the ground. Like everything else, the floor was cold and damp but it felt quite refreshing. It felt so nice to relax my legs and I sat there in a daze. My mind went back to when I was little, I would always run around like a headless chicken, and sitting down afterwards was the highlight of my life; clearly things haven't changed.

Finally, I see a light approaching me. This has to be the nurse coming back for me. I stood up quickly, I don't want her to think I have been laying around. If I make out that I am scared then maybe they will go easy on me. She walked fast paced and her faint heels clanked as they strode across the echoing floor. She approached me, gave me the light, and told me to follow her.

I could just about see where I was going now I had control of the light. We walked down a very thin corridor with high walls which appeared to have graffiti all over them, it was too dark to make out what the words said and I wasn't really in the state of mind to be concentrating on stuff like that right now. We came to a wooden door with about 7 locks and bolts barricading it shut, the nurse pushed the door open and pushed me in, she blew out my light and closed the door. I can't even explain what this room looks like as I cannot see a thing, however it feels tense and bitter and I am not comfortable. I didn't know anything about the contents of this room or the size to be able to navigate my way to somewhere safe. As far as I am concerned, I am not moving from this spot. I mean, I've been standing here for a few minutes now and nothing has killed me yet, so I guess this is the safe zone. I wonder if this is where I will be staying the whole time? To be fair though, it was pretty late in the day by the time the nurse reappeared back here, so maybe this is just temporary until they can sort something more permanent out in the morning.

Making sure I stayed in the same spot the whole way down, I sat cross legged with my hands in my lap, I didn't want to risk anything touching me like a rat or something so I curled myself up in a ball on the floor, closed my eyes, and wished the world away.

Surprisingly enough, I slept like a baby. I always do sleep well when it is cold though so I guess that worked to my advantage. I opened my eyes and looked at what was in front of me. The room was filthy; the walls were stained sky high with dirt and what looks to me like dry blood. Written in thick, black capital letters in the middle of the wall before me was a paragraph that said:

"FOR WE DO NOT RESIGNATE OURSELVES
TO HE WHO WILL ONLY TAKE ADVANTAGE,
MAY YOUR BLOOD RUN DEEP,
AND YOUR THOUGHTS RUN WILD.
IT IS BETTER TO ASK FOR THE WORLD
THAN TO TAKE IT
BUT WHAT IF NOBODY EVER ASKS?
LIVING IS FOR THE ABNORMAL,
DYING IS FOR THE INSPIRATIONAL.
I'LL CLOSE MY OWN FUCKING COFFIN
BEFORE YOU TAKE ME FOR SLANDER.
YOU DO NOT OWN ME ,
NOR WILL YOU EVER.
IF I DIE HERE,
WHICH I WILL.
AT LEAST I WONT HAVE TO SEE YOU ROT IN HELL!"

There has always been something about things like that which give me Goosebumps to read. It's the passion. Scary regardless, but powerful. What has gone on in this room to account for such a pessimistic verse like That?

Other than the strongly worded verse on the wall, the room was empty and dull. The floor was grey with black trainer marks all over it, and there was a window in one of the corners with bars around it. Not much different from my other room with regards to decor, obviously the lack of a bed was a big difference, but the floor was probably just as comfy. The first thing I did realise however was that there was no toilet. Not even a bucket. I am quite happy I hadn't had much to drink because usually I would be busting by now. There wasn't anything else to do other than sit and wait to see if anything will happen to me. There is a possibility that I will be left to starve or dehydrate, they said that no one leaves here alive and I highly doubt that they will be prioritising my health or well-being.

Chapter 24

I guess one good thing has come out of this though, I don't have to eat that crappy canteen food anymore or put up with those vulgar serving ladies. You always have to see a silver lining in each situation in order to stop yourself from going into a state of destruction or delusion which causes you to wish ways out of things that you may be able to overcome. Well that is how I always see things anyway. If you have at least one positive thing in your mind to focus on, then it doesn't matter about the bad stuff as much. Optimism is something that if everyone possessed, the world would initially be a more accepting place and more comforting to live in. Democracy is too valued in the sense that the things politicians stand for or believe are priorities for the country are just merely unnecessary ideas and schemes to con everyone for their money. Emigration is something that this country suffers with, and as long as the people coming over here make our country money, they aren't exactly going to be rushing to fix the problem anytime soon. Its basically double standards, you restrain people from getting jobs because emigrants work for less money than we do, but then you prosecute people for claiming benefits without a valid reason, when the reason is that there physically is not enough jobs and that is something that the government need to take control over. I tend to rant a lot about things that I can't myself physically change, but I, being a living citizen in this situation believe that they should focus on everyone's point of view. When it comes to elections and voting, I think that if there are a lot of votes for each that they should tie everybody's ideas together to make it fair and more just. And don't even get me started on some of the laws that are in place these days.

Chapter 25

My inclinations again were correct. The nurse came around midday, I guessed by the sun beams position coming through the window. She opened the door, gave me half a baguette and told me to eat quickly because we don't have a lot of time.

A lot of time for what?

I ate it quickly, but not because she told me to. Hunger was taking over my body and I knew I needed some energy if I was going to be taken to somewhere else. I stood up, stretched and continued out of the room. This basement place obviously has a set temperature as I was still freezing. This place didn't look as scary now though, I mean I still could hardly see anything but what I did see seemed normal and not as alarming as once thought. Your mind can be very evil and to be honest I don't think that I am really in the mood to be giving a shit about a few blood stains up a wall.

This walk was shorter, I felt like I was walking to a prison cell. Ironic huh? Once again not a word from the nurse was spoken until we came to a metal door which had a scratched sign on it saying "lawmoot" I am not particularly strong with knowledge when it comes to old words but I'm pretty sure that a lawmoot is the word for some kind of court room or legal office, well it used to be anyway. Clearly that is not what is behind this door so it's going to be a guessing game like everything else here.

"It didn't have to be this way you know Miss Leslie." she said softly but with a stern look on her face. I looked at her innocently. "If the days would change but the hours stayed still, would the sun not rise because the shadow of the moon is taking its place in the sky? Determination requires strength and control, and if anything, I will go down who I am, and not someone you wanted me to be"

"This will be the last time you see me Charlotte, I am not in charge of your care anymore, and it is a different system down here. There are things you will see and learn that will really test your strength.

How it will go is based on how you treat the situations and problems if and when they occur. Leave it as it may, good luck." she smirked and proceeded with opening the door.

"You know what? You're a good person nurse. You helped me feel safe in a place that was capitalizing my thoughts and capturing my devotion to myself and trying to turn it into self loathe. And for that I will always be grateful." I smiled at her, walked through the door and heard it slam shut behind me.

18165074R00033

Printed in Great Britain
by Amazon